THE
ORPHANED
TIGER

tiger tales

5 River Road, Suite 128, Wilton, CT 06897
Published in the United States 2023
Originally published as 'Star' in Great Britain in 2019
by Little Tiger Press Limited
Text copyright © 2019 Holly Webb
Illustrations copyright © 2019 Artful Doodlers
Cover illustrations copyright © 2023 Simon Mendez
Author photograph copyright © Charlotte Knee Photography
Photographic images courtesy of www.shutterstock.com
ISBN-13: 978-1-6643-4061-9
ISBN-10: 1-6643-4061-0
Printed in China
STP/3800/0516/0423

www.tigertalesbooks.com

THE ORPHANED TIGER

by HOLLY WEBB

tiger tales

For all my readers in Russia—
thank you for the wonderful welcome
you gave me when I visited!

~ HOLLY WEBB

Contents

Chapter
ONE

Baba's Tiger

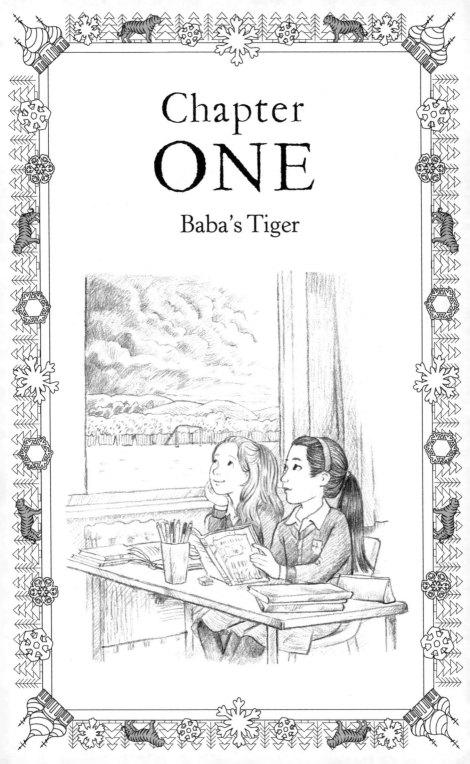

"Do you really think it will snow?" Anna whispered as soon as Mr. Ford's back was turned. They were supposed to be reading, but most of the class had at least one eye on the window and the patch of yellowish-gray sky they could see over the wall of the playground.

"Definitely," Ruby whispered back. "It's so cold. And it just looks like snow, doesn't it?"

Anna nodded. There was something about that scrap of sky. It looked heavy, as if the clouds were filled with snow. Just in time for the end of the semester tomorrow. It would be perfect. She peered over her page at the clock—surely it was dismissal time by now! Usually she loved ending the day with reading, but the thought of snow made it too hard to concentrate.

When the bell rang at last, there was a second of complete silence and then everyone leaped up, cramming books and pencil cases into their backpacks and racing for the door.

"If it snows like it's supposed to, maybe we won't even have to come to school tomorrow," Ruby said hopefully.

"The last day's always fun, though!" Anna said, wrapping a scarf around her neck. "Mr. Ford said we can watch a DVD after lunch. But that's not as much fun as playing in the snow," she admitted.

"Exactly! Come on, let's go and see if it's started yet!"

Anna and Ruby hurried out onto the playground to look at the sky. It was a dark, dark gray now, but there were still no snowflakes.

"Do you think the forecast was wrong?" Ruby said, peering at the clouds.

Anna sighed. "I hope not."

"It will snow, *zvezda moya*, don't worry."

"Baba!" Anna turned to hug her grandma. "I forgot you were picking me up today. Mom's going to her office Christmas party and Dad's working," she explained to Ruby. "I'm staying over at Baba's house tonight."

Ruby nodded. "What does *zvez*— whatever your baba said, mean?" she whispered.

"It's Russian for 'my star,'" Anna explained. "It's just a nice thing to call somebody. Baba, do you really think it's going to snow?"

"Definitely. Those are snow clouds.

If it doesn't start before you go to bed tonight, you will wake up to a white world tomorrow, I'm certain. Now—" she looked thoughtfully at Anna's bag—"do you have everything? Your mama dropped a bag off with me this morning, but she said to make sure you had brought everything home. Homework? PE uniform?"

"No homework and I have my PE uniform." Anna waved it in front of her.

"See you tomorrow, Anna! My mom's calling me." Ruby dashed away, and Anna slipped her hand into Baba's.

"Can we watch a movie together tonight?"

"Mmm, I should think so. You can find us a nice Christmas movie. I made those honey cookies you like. We can have some when we get home."

They walked back to Baba's house, admiring all the Christmas lights and decorations on the way. Anna liked the sparkling reindeer standing on her neighbor's lawn.

"We're going to put up our tree this weekend. Do you have a tree yet, Baba?"

"My little tinsel tree is in the attic, but I haven't brought it down yet. Maybe you can help me put it up later. But it feels early to me to be putting up a tree. Christmas is weeks away," Baba grumbled, and Anna laughed.

The church in Russia worked on a different calendar, so Christmas Day wasn't until January 7. There would be all the New Year celebrations first. Anna loved the party that Baba always had for all her Russian friends on New Year's Eve.

"You could always have Christmas twice!" Anna suggested.

"Two Christmases! Certainly not." Baba shook her head, pretending to be annoyed. "What an idea. You know, your cousins in Russia won't be on their school break until the day before New Year's Eve."

Anna sighed. "I bet Tatiana and Peter and Annushka have tons of snow."

"Oh, yes." Baba smiled. "But nothing like a year or so ago, when they had that huge snowfall. Do you remember? Two months' worth of snow fell in one night, and Uncle Michael had to dig out their front door."

"I wish we could go and visit them again," Anna said enviously. "But in the winter, this time. We could go to Russia for New Year! I'd love to see really deep snow. Here it's just cold." She shivered. It was definitely a lot colder than it had been the day before.

They hurried into Baba's little

apartment, and Baba made a cup of tea for herself and hot chocolate for Anna. Dipping the spiced honey cookies into the hot chocolate, Anna started to feel her frozen toes again. "This is nice, Baba," she said. But she couldn't resist looking around to check out the window for snow.

"It will come, Anna! I promise. Let's go and watch our movie, okay?"

It was wonderful, snuggled up on the couch. Anna almost forgot about the snow. She was starting to feel really Christmassy now.

What should she get Baba for Christmas? she wondered as the movie ended and Baba went into the kitchen to heat up the soup she'd made for dinner. Baba loved little ornaments. She had a lot of them on the shelves in her living room—

animals and dancing girls and baskets of flowers. Maybe she could buy her grandma a special new one.

"Anna, switch it over to the news, please," Baba called from the kitchen. "I like to know what's going on. I can hear it from here."

Anna changed channels and went on looking at Baba's ornaments, wondering whether she had enough allowance to buy something really nice. Then something on the television caught her attention, and she yelped with excitement.

"What is it?" Baba asked, popping her head around the door.

"Look! It's Vladivostok! That's near where Tatiana and Peter and Annushka live, isn't it? It's on the news!"

"I'll turn the soup down." Baba hurried

back into the kitchen and then came to sit with Anna. "What's happening? Is it the snow again?"

"No! They're saying there's a tiger in the city!"

"Oh, my.... I don't believe it." Baba peered at the screen, gasping at the blurry footage of a tiger—a real tiger!—racing across a busy road.

"They're trying to catch him," Anna explained. "And they've given him a name—Vladik, like the city. Did you ever see a tiger when you lived near Vladivostok, Baba?"

"Never," her baba replied. "Tigers are wild, so they never usually come near people. Even in our tiny village close to the forest we never saw one. Right into the city? It's hard to believe."

"I hope the tiger's okay," Anna said thoughtfully. "I bet he was scared of those cars."

Baba nodded, and then sighed as the news program showed footage of police tracking the tiger. "And now he has all these people chasing him...."

"They won't hurt him, will they?" Anna asked worriedly. "He's so beautiful—but I suppose it would be really scary if he got into a supermarket or something."

"Oh!" Baba took her phone out of her pocket. "It's your mama. She probably wants to say good night to you before she goes to the party. Hello, Maria!"

"Can I tell her about the tiger, Baba, please?" Anna asked excitedly.

"Maria, you'll not believe what we just saw on the news. Here, Anna will tell you." Baba passed over the phone, and Anna grabbed it eagerly.

"Mom! There's a tiger loose in Vladivostok! A wild tiger!"

"Wow! What's it doing there?"

"No one knows—they said on the news that maybe it was looking for food. They're trying to catch him to take him back to the forest."

"Tigers are really rare," her mom said. "But I suppose with towns getting bigger they will end up coming closer to people. I expect they're doing everything they can to catch him safely, Anna, don't worry. Are you having fun with Baba? Did she make honey cookies for you?"

"Yes. And we watched a movie."

"Lucky you. Sleep well, okay? Last day of school tomorrow."

"Have fun at the party, Mom!" Anna handed back the phone and heard Baba and Mom switch to Russian. Anna knew some Russian, but not enough to understand Baba when she was talking fast. She went back to looking at Baba's ornaments. Most of them were animals, she realized. Anna had played with some of them before— there was a whole family of beautiful bears, the littlest one not much bigger than the end of Anna's thumb. She loved arranging them, and she'd given them all names long ago. But behind the bears, looking a little bit dusty, was another creature, long and low with a beautiful heavy curl of tail.

Anna picked up the wooden figure, wondering how she'd never noticed it before. It was a tiger, but it looked plumper than the one on the news, small, and a little fluffy, as if it were a cub. The woodcarver had used some kind of special wood with a clear grain to it, so even though the tiger wasn't painted, it still had beautiful stripes.

"Ah, you found my little tiger!" Baba came over to see what Anna was holding. "He's beautiful, isn't he?"

"Where did he come from, Baba?"

Baba smiled. "Your Uncle Michael made him for me—he's very good at carving animals, and he made the little bears, too. Your cousin Annushka has a tiger just like this one, and when I said how beautiful it was, Michael made one for me."

Anna smiled. She had only met Annushka once, but they spoke on the phone sometimes. They were almost exactly the same age, and they had the same name—Annushka was a pet name for Anna. She wondered what Annushka was doing right now—had she seen the news about the tiger in

Vladivostok, too?

Anna put the tiger in the middle of the kitchen table while they were eating their soup, and when it was time for bed, she looked pleadingly at Baba. "Could I take him with me? He reminds me of Vladik, the tiger on the news. I can't stop thinking about him."

"Of course you can." Baba hugged her. "And don't worry, Anna. I am sure the tiger will be all right."

Anna had just put on her pajamas when Baba called from the living room. "Anna! Look out the window, *zvezda moya!*"

Anna hurried across the room and drew back the curtains. "It's snowing!" she whispered delightedly. A few fat heavy flakes were floating down, glowing in the light of the street lamp.

"Do you think there'll be more?" she said as Baba came to stand behind her. "Will it stick?"

"I'm sure it will. Go to bed—you'll catch a cold standing there staring at it!"

"Will you come and talk to me for a while?" Anna pleaded. "You could tell me about my cousins and their village." She loved it when Baba told her stories about life in Russia.

"It's getting late," Baba grumbled, but she came and sat on the end of Anna's bed anyway. "Do you want to hear about the snow again, *zvezda moya?*"

"Yes, please," Anna said sleepily.

"Okay, well…. Did you know, Annushka once went outside in the snow without her warm hood on, and it was so cold that her eyelashes froze?"

"That's silly, Baba. You're making it up…."

"Not at all. You have to be careful when it's that cold. And now with tigers out there, too. I will call your aunt, tell her to make sure they all stay close to the house. Are you asleep, Anna?"

"Mmmm…."

"Good night then, Annushka!" Baba leaned over to give her a kiss and then padded away, her footsteps tiger-soft.

Anna smiled to herself. She loved it when Baba called her that. Yawning, she rolled over and looked at the wooden tiger standing guard on the little chest of drawers beside the bed. He was carved with a snarl and he looked fierce, but Anna thought maybe he was scared. She snuggled under the comforter, wishing she'd brought her really warm pajamas. Sleepily, she reached out to hold the little wooden tiger, tucking him next to her cheek.

Not really fierce, she thought, as her eyes drifted shut again and the tiger cub slunk away down the street outside Baba's apartment, shaking the snowflakes from his whiskers.

Chapter
TWO

Tiger on the Loose

It was even colder when Anna woke up, and she huddled the bedcovers over her head to make a warm little cave with her breath. Maybe Baba's heating hadn't come on, she thought. It had never been this cold when she'd slept over at Baba's before. Or maybe the snow had kept on falling and falling the night before. Maybe they were snowed in, like Tatiana and Peter and Annushka had been in their village.

Anna threw back the covers and bounced out of bed to look, but her room was so dark she could hardly see. It must be earlier than she'd thought. She picked her way across to the window and drew back the curtains. The snow was everywhere, piled up against the walls and glimmering in the purplish light of early morning.

And it wasn't just the snow and the

eerie light that was making everything look different, Anna realized, her fingers closing tightly on the curtain. The view from the window had changed. There was no road outside, no line of houses facing her window. Instead, there were trees— tall dark pine trees laced with snow.

A movement behind Anna made her whirl around, and she saw that the door of her bedroom was opening.

"Oh, you're up already, Annushka."

Anna stared at the woman in the doorway. Everything in her head seemed suddenly clouded and confused. She was Anna, getting ready for the last day of school, excited that snow had started falling at last. But she was also Annushka, who didn't think snow was all that special. It just meant the house was much colder, and she couldn't play outside for as long as she could in the summer. Annushka had been waking up to darkness and snow for weeks and weeks.

Anna blinked, and her mama gave her a hug and then turned to go over to the other bed—the one that Anna hadn't even noticed. "Tatiana, are you awake? I'm making *syrniki*, girls. Hurry and get dressed while I go and wake up Peter. You need something nice and hot on such a cold day."

Syrniki were Annushka's favorite— little pancakes with creamy cheese in the mixture. She started getting dressed at once. She wasn't sure what she had been dreaming about last night, but it had left her feeling odd, as though she had to think about everything twice before she did it.

Annushka slid into her seat at the kitchen table, sniffing happily at the smell of frying pancakes. Her mama passed her a plate with little round pancakes on it, and Annushka added jam and a spoonful of sour cream. Tatiana wandered in yawning, with Peter after her. They both brightened up when they saw the *syrniki*. Mama passed out more plates and sat down at the table with them.

"Listen to me, you three. You must be careful when you're outside today."

"Why? Because it's so cold?" Annushka asked through a mouthful of pancake. She looked worriedly at the plate in the middle of the table. There weren't many pancakes left and Peter was taking a bunch....

Mama shook her head. "It is cold today, but that's not the reason. Eva's father saw a tiger last night."

Annushka let her fork fall onto her plate in surprise. Eva was her friend who lived a few houses away, on the edge of the forest.

Peter looked disbelieving. "A tiger? What, while he was out hunting in the forest? But no one sees tigers, or hardly ever, anyway."

"I know. And he wasn't even in the

forest. He was taking firewood from the shed into the house. The tiger walked past the back of the shed. Or so he says."

Annushka wasn't sure whether her mama believed Eva's father or not. She sounded a bit doubtful, and Annushka was, too. Tigers were so rare, and they were really shy of people. A few of the hunters in the village said they'd seen tigers in the forest, or thought they had, but it was very unusual. They saw bears much more often and wild boar sometimes, too.

"Anyway ... just in case, make sure you stay with the others today, won't you? Don't go off anywhere on your own."

Annushka nodded, and as her mama cleared away the plates and glasses, she reached into the pocket of her cardigan and drew out a wooden tiger, turning it over in her hands. It was just a little toy that her papa had carved for her—he liked to whittle a piece of wood to keep his hands busy in the evenings after they'd eaten dinner, and he had made her so many beautiful wooden animals. Annushka had a whole line of them on the shelf in her bedroom, but this tiger was her favorite. Papa had carved it for her after they had read a book of old folktales, and Annushka had wanted the story about the girl who turned into a tiger over and over again.

She loved the way the grain of the wood shone like the tiger's striped coat. Papa carved all kinds of things, but the animals and birds he made were the best. He spent a while watching wild creatures, and it showed in the carvings he made.

For a moment Annushka saw her wooden tiger on a different shelf, next to a china basket of flowers she'd certainly never owned. Then she shook her head, flicking away the daydream. She tucked the tiger back into her pocket. She could hear footsteps outside—that would be Eva, coming to get them, ready to walk to school.

"Did you hear about the tiger?" Eva shouted as Annushka clumped out of the door in her boots. "Papa saw one! It almost ate him!"

"I thought it just walked behind the woodshed," Annushka said doubtfully.

"It was enormous," Eva said, ignoring her. "He's just lucky it didn't attack. It was so close."

"What if it comes back?" Tatiana said. "We shouldn't stay outside too long. Not if there's a tiger hanging around. It has to be here for food, doesn't it? We'd better hurry up and get to school."

"Are there tracks, Eva?" Annushka asked curiously. "Can you see the tiger's paw prints by your woodshed?"

"I don't think so—it snowed again last night. But we could pop back and take a look, just in case," Eva suggested hopefully.

"Mama said we have to stick together," Peter said firmly. "And keep well away from the forest. The tiger could be really close."

"But we would be away from the forest!" Eva said. "Our woodshed isn't near the forest, not that near anyway, and we'd be together. A tiger isn't going to attack us if we're all in a group, is it? Aren't you curious?"

"No." Peter shook his head grimly.

"Tigers are huge. My grandfather has a tiger's tooth, he showed it to me and Tatiana."

"What about me?" Annushka asked. She didn't remember seeing a tooth.

"You were too little," Peter said crushingly. "I don't want to be anywhere near an actual tiger. It's looking for easy prey, Eva. Careless prey, like you going hunting for tiger prints when you've been told not to."

Eva started to argue, but Tatiana was nodding determinedly, and she wasn't brave enough to go off on her own. So Eva grabbed a mittenful of snow and tried to sling it at Peter, but she missed, and then she started to laugh, giggling at herself and hurling snowballs at all three of them.

Annushka sighed a little, even as she joined in the snowball fight. She knew Peter was right, really. It wasn't that she meant to ignore their mama and risk being hurt by a tiger, but they were such rare and beautiful creatures, even if they were dangerous. She couldn't help feeling that it would be magical to see a tiger slipping in between the trees.

Everyone at school had heard about the tiger, and Eva was mobbed as soon as they walked in. Even their teachers wanted to know more, and Eva and Annushka's class spent half an English lesson trying to talk about tigers and how fierce they were. All the chasing games at lunch were suddenly called Tiger in the Forest or The Tiger's Coming, and people kept popping around corners and roaring at each other. By dismissal time, everyone was excited and giggly and enjoying being a little scared.

Annushka and the others usually walked home in a big group, chatting and messing around, but today everyone was stomping along fast. It was just too cold to be outside for long, and the snow was very deep. Even though paths had been dug through the drifts so people could walk through the village, it was still slippery and hard to see. Besides, even in their coats and boots and mittens, the cold cut straight through.

Annushka walked back to her house with her brother and sister and Eva and a couple of others, sticking together like they'd been told. None of them really expected to see a tiger, though. They'd spent the day laughing about the story, and many of the older children had said Eva's father must have been mistaken—it was a deer he saw, or maybe a bear. Tigers were in the old folktales they'd learned in school. The Udege people used to think that tigers were the spirit of the forest.

That didn't fit into a world of phones and TVs and computers.

So when Eva picked up a handful of snow and started creeping up behind Peter with a wicked look on her face, no one told her to stop. They shot away in all directions, ducking behind each other and scooping up more snow. Annushka hurled a snowball and caught Tatiana right on the side of her hood, and her big sister grabbed a handful of snow and called, "I'm going to get you!"

Annushka didn't even think before she dashed off ahead.

"You're too slow!" she yelled back, turning to make faces at Tatiana and the others. "Come on! Try to catch me!"

The snow was tightly packed under Annushka's boots as she charged along.

She could hear Tatiana and the others chasing her, but they were falling behind. Annushka shot out of the pathway through a deep drift, not far from Eva's house, closer to the woods. She stood with her hands on her knees, panting and laughing to herself. The others were way behind, and she was all by herself for a moment.

It was as she straightened up that she caught a glimpse of something moving in the trees behind her. A glint of rusty-orange fur standing out against the snow and the dark branches.

Annushka's heart stood still—it felt like it really had stopped. She certainly wasn't breathing. She froze, like a statue, too terrified to move, let alone run away. While she was standing there, her mind raced. Was it better to be still? If she ran, wouldn't that just make the tiger chase her? Maybe it wasn't a tiger after all. It could be anything—a plastic bag flapping in the wind, or ... or....

No. It was definitely a tiger. As Annushka stood and stared, the creature stepped forward, gazing back at her. But this was no great, terrifying beast, its teeth bared, about to leap on her and drag her away.

It was a cub—half grown at most.

That didn't mean it wasn't dangerous, of course. Annushka knew it still had claws like knives, and razor-sharp teeth. The tiger growled, low in its throat, and Annushka shivered with fright. But the cub didn't come any closer, or show its teeth. It stood pressed against a tree, gazing at her.

It looked ... worried. Or even frightened,
Annushka thought, her racing heartbeats
slowing. The dazed, cold feeling inside

her eased a little, and she started to be able to think again. The cub wasn't just small. She was almost sure it was too thin. It didn't look like the well-fed tiger she had seen at the zoo in Vladivostok. It was skinny, and its coat was dirty and dull. It looked like it needed a mother tiger to give it a good bath. She giggled, mostly out of fright. The cub cringed back behind the tree, and Annushka gasped. It was scared of *her*.

"I'm sorry," she whispered. "I didn't mean to frighten you. I really didn't."

She looked into the cub's golden eyes for the first time, and saw that they were wide and worried in their edging of white fur. They gazed at each other, silent and still, and then Annushka stepped a little closer.

"What is it? What's wrong? You shouldn't be here, you know—you're too close to the village. It's dangerous." She saw the cub's ears flicker and it glanced sideways, and then she heard the voices of the others, high and anxious. They were calling for her.

"Annushka! Annushka! Where are you?"

"Annushka, answer us!"

"Annushka, are you okay?"

She looked around to see if they were close … and when she looked back, the cub was gone. She couldn't even see the tip of its tail. *Her tail*, Annushka thought. In that moment when they had looked into each other's eyes, she had felt sure the cub was a girl, frightened and alone, just as she was.

Annushka wished they'd had longer together. The only sign that a tiger had been there was a faint trail of paw prints, leading away between the trees. Without even thinking about it, she scuffed over the nearest prints with her boot.

"Annushka! Where did you go? Why did you run off like that?" Eva came dashing out of the snowdrift path, her face red from running and the cold. "We were worried about you!"

"You shouldn't have gone off on your own," Peter told her angrily, but she could tell he was only angry because he was frightened. "We're not supposed to go into the forest, and especially not today!"

"I'm sorry," she muttered. "But...."

"But what?" Peter snapped.

"Nothing.... Don't fuss. I didn't go into

the forest, did I? Look—I can't touch a single tree from here."

She'd been about to tell them she'd seen the tiger and it was just a cub, not a huge man-eating terror. But she didn't— the words just wouldn't come. If she told the others that a tiger had wandered so close to the village again, everyone would panic. Many of the men in the village went hunting for deer, and almost every household had a gun. It would take only one hunter to decide he needed to protect his family from the tiger....

No, she had to keep quiet, to keep the tiger safe. But most of all, Annushka wanted to keep that moment where she and the cub had looked into each other's eyes.

Chapter
THREE

Annushka's Decision

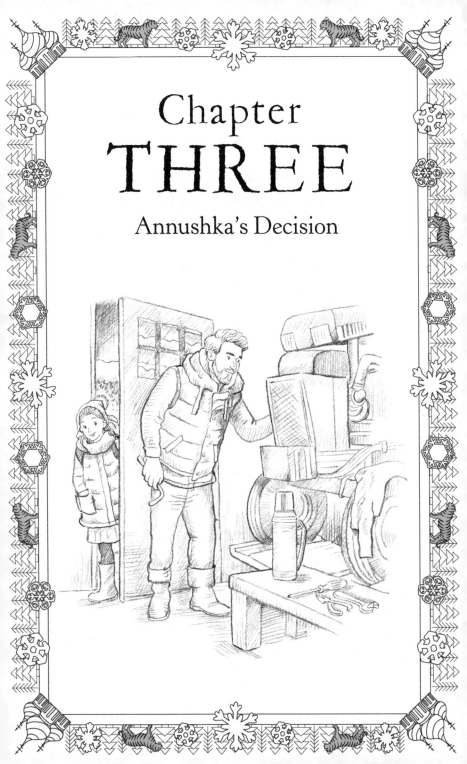

When they got back, Annushka slipped into her papa's workshop—he was a mechanic and fixed all the cars and farm equipment for miles around—and rushed to ask him for news about the tiger. Every time anyone dropped into the workshop, they always chatted for a while. Her papa loved to talk, and he always had the most up-to-date gossip in the village.

"Slow down, slow down, let me give you a hug first.... Hmm.... Where's your mama, Annushka? Does she know you're back home?"

"She just popped next door to ask Nastya about something. But Papa, has there been any more news about the tiger? Has anyone else seen her? It, I mean?" Annushka turned pink, hoping he hadn't noticed her slip.

Annushka's papa laughed. "Half the village has seen it, if you believe what I've been hearing today. But I spoke to Eva's father, and he thinks it was a young one, not much more than a cub, and definitely not fully grown." He sighed. "Poor creature. Dimitri came in this afternoon—you know, the vet? He thinks the tiger would only be this close to the houses if there was something wrong and it was desperate for food. He thinks maybe it's been injured by poachers."

Annushka shook her head. "Poachers! But tigers are protected! No one's supposed to hunt them."

"I know." Her papa reached out and put an arm around Annushka's shoulders. "Not everyone thinks tigers are special the way you do, though. There are people who still hunt them—they can make a lot of money from it, sadly. Dealers will pay a fortune for tiger teeth and claws; they use them in folk remedies."

He shook his head. "When I told Dimitri that Eva's father thought the tiger was a young one, he said it's possible that poachers killed a mother tiger and this is her cub. They're not so good at hunting when they're small, you see—the mother hunts for them. This one might not be able to feed itself with its mother gone."

Annushka thought of the skinny tiger she'd seen that afternoon. She had felt sorry for the cub before, but now that she knew it could be an orphan, it was much worse.

"What will happen?" she asked her papa anxiously. "Is there anything we can do to help? Maybe we could put some food out for it, if it's hungry and doesn't know how to hunt?"

Her papa opened his flask of tea and took a long swallow. The steam wreathed around his face, and he closed his eyes. "Ah, that's better. What do you think will happen if we put food out for a hungry tiger, Annushka?"

"It won't be hungry anymore!" Annushka said, shrugging. She sat down on the bench next to her papa and leaned against him.

"Mmm. For how long?"

Annushka stopped to think and frowned. "I ... don't know," she admitted. "I'm not sure how often tigers eat. Maybe a couple of days?"

"And then should we feed the tiger again?" her papa asked gently.

"Well ... yes! Or ... I don't know." Annushka nibbled the end of her braid. She thought tigers probably ate quite a lot, and mostly meat. It could get very expensive to keep feeding a tiger. "But we'd only have to put out food until it learned to hunt for itself," she said.

"How is the tiger going to do that, with no mother to teach it? Especially when *we're* teaching it to come to a place where food just magically appears, and it doesn't have to do anything for it."

"I see what you mean," Annushka said slowly.

Her papa sipped his tea. "And then maybe one day someone might forget to feed the tiger, or maybe they can't because they're not very well—then what have you got?"

Annushka sank her chin onto her hands. "A hungry tiger."

"A hungry, desperate tiger, who can't hunt properly. But it's learned to come to a village full of people for food. People who aren't afraid of the tiger because they see it often now, so they don't take care and they don't know they need to run."

"All right." Annushka nodded. "I understand what you're saying, Papa. But we can't just leave the poor tiger cub to starve!"

"No, of course not. Dimitri told me he's already contacted a special nature reserve to let them know we've had a tiger sighting. They said that if the tiger stays around here, they'll come and trap it and take it back to the reserve. They're experts. They can teach tigers how to be wild again. They've had a lot of success releasing rewilded creatures."

He stood up and stretched his arms above his head with a groan. "Come on, *zvezda moya*. I need more than tea to keep me going. Let's see if your mama needs some help making dinner."

"So, we have to watch out for the tiger and let them know?" Annushka asked hopefully as they came through the door that connected the workshop with the back of the house. Tatiana and Peter were in the living room— she could hear the TV.

"You're not watching out for anything," her father said firmly. "Even if it's a young tiger, it's still very dangerous."

The front door thumped and Annushka heard her mama coming in, shaking the snow off her boots and muttering about how cold it was. "What's very dangerous?" she asked as she came into the kitchen, pulling on a warm pair of slippers.

"This tiger. I was just telling Annushka that maybe someone from the nature reserve will be able to come and trap it."

Mama shuddered. "I was nervous even going from Nastya's door to ours. I hope they come and take it away soon."

"She's only a cub, Mama!" Annushka protested. "Please don't talk about her like that."

"She?" Mama smiled at her. "Annushka ... we don't know the tiger is even a cub, let alone a girl."

In her head, Annushka was saying, *But she is, she is!* Out loud all she said was, "Eva's father said it was a cub. He saw it."

"Ah!" Mama nodded, looking relieved. "Well, that's good. I'm sure a cub isn't as dangerous as a full-grown tiger."

"Dimitri the vet thinks the cub's mother was killed," Annushka explained, her voice shaking a little. "And now she's all alone."

"Oh...." Annushka's mother looked a little shocked. "Oh, that is sad."

"It means the tiger's desperate for food," Papa said gently. "I know you think a tiger cub looks cute, Annushka, and this one's hungry and it's all very sad—but a tiger cub isn't like a kitten. It could still hurt you very badly."

Annushka nodded, but she couldn't

look at her papa. Most of her knew that he was right—but a tiny part, deep inside, remembered the tiger's frightened golden eyes.

"Is anyone from the village going to go and look for the tiger?" she asked hopefully. "Dimitri, maybe? Wouldn't it be better to try and find her, so we can tell the people from the nature reserve to come. I mean—" she swallowed hard—"if she doesn't know how to hunt, she must be starving. It's cruel to leave her on her own out there."

Papa shook his head. "Zvezda moya, even Dimitri isn't an expert on tigers. No one is going to put themselves at risk like that—it's just asking for trouble. The nature reserve staff has special equipment—tranquilizers and I don't know what else.

They know how to approach a tiger. It's not something we can do."

"So we're not going to do anything?" Annushka whispered. If she'd tried to talk any louder, she would have cried.

That night, Annushka lay in bed with the little wooden tiger pressed tightly into her hand. The sharp ruff of fur carved around the tiger's head was hurting her, but she couldn't seem to loosen her grip. What was she going to do? She had seen the tiger cub, but then she hadn't told anyone. She had wanted to keep that amazing moment all to herself. She had let the tiger cub turn and walk away among the gathering trees.

If she'd said something, maybe the people from the nature reserve would think it worth coming to the village. But it was too late to say anything now. The cub might still be close to the village, or she could be miles away. Annushka had missed the chance to help her.

She would have to do something else instead. Even after everything Papa had said about how dangerous tigers were, Annushka knew she had to go out there and find the cub. She had been told many times she must never go into the forest on her own—that it was easy to get lost, and it was full of wild creatures.

She shivered. She didn't want to go, but something was telling her she must. Just not yet. Not while her mama and papa were still awake. No, she was going to have to wait until it was truly nighttime and she could sneak out without being heard. She needed to search the kitchen, and maybe even Papa's workshop, so that she was ready.

Annushka peered over at Tatiana, making sure her sister was already asleep. Then she reached into the drawer of the table by her bed and pulled out her flashlight and a notebook with a pencil on a string.

She needed a list, if she was really going to do this. She pulled the covers over her head and switched on the flashlight so they made a little glowing cave. She began to write, stopping every so often to nibble the edge of her thumbnail. Even thinking about going out in the snow all alone was making her nervous.

Flashlight

Warm clothes

A first-aid kit? Did they have one of those? Maybe just some bandages....

Food—for me and the tiger

Annushka caught her breath anxiously and scribbled on.

Two pairs of gloves

A map? When they'd gone walking in the forest with Papa and Mama, they hadn't had a map, but Papa had explained they were keeping to marked paths and they weren't actually going far from the village.

Annushka had a feeling that tigers didn't walk on marked paths. She sighed and peered at her watch. Her parents had gone to bed an hour or so before—Mama had looked around the door and mumbled, "Sleep well, *zvezda moya.*"

She had heard them moving around in their room for a little while, but all was quiet now—except for an occasional snuffly snore from her papa. It was eleven o'clock, and the house was very still.

How much longer should she wait before she walked out into the forest to go looking for a tiger?

Chapter
FOUR

A Nighttime Adventure

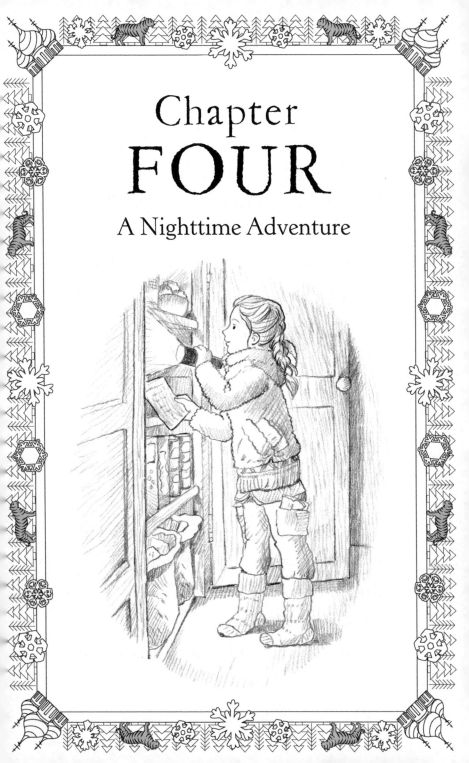

The little room grew colder and colder as the night wore on. Annushka huddled under her bedsheets, trying to find the courage to move.

She had been curled up in her bed for what felt like hours now, worrying and planning and trying to think if this was a bad idea. Actually, she *knew* it was a bad idea, but she wanted to do it anyway. Even though her sensible side said she should listen to her parents, her friends, and everyone else in the village. That she shouldn't be going anywhere near a tiger.

But there had been something so lost in the cub's golden eyes. Annushka was determined to find her.

Moving as quietly as she could, Annushka crept out of bed and began to dress, with one eye cautiously on her sleeping sister. She needed as many layers as she could possibly put on—vests, long-sleeved shirts, a sweater. Three pairs of warm socks. Her boots were good waterproof ones, and she'd take two pairs of thick gloves and her fluffy furry hat. It didn't matter if she looked like a snowman, as long as she kept warm. She could get frostbite if she was out there in the cold too long.

Her grandfather had lost two toes to frostbite a few years before—he said he hadn't even realized it was happening. He had shown her the stumps and Annushka shuddered, remembering. Then she padded downstairs to the kitchen and started to fill her pockets with supplies, squinting at her list.

She picked up her coat as she slipped out through the door and onto the porch, and wrapped a huge scarf around her face as one last layer. Then she gripped her flashlight tightly, her fingers swollen by the double layer of gloves.

The beam of light shone out onto the packed snow—at least it was a clear night, with no more snow falling. But the light seemed so thin and faint. It hardly cut through the darkness at all. She was only about a hundred yards from the trees and there the darkness seemed even thicker, a heavy mass of black on black.

Annushka stood hesitating on the porch, listening to the sounds of the sleeping village. The creak of wooden houses shifting in the wind. A faint sigh from someone's stove, keeping the house warm through the night. A dog turning over in its sleep with a breath of a growl. That was all. She was the only one awake.

As she reached behind her for the handle of the door, Annushka wasn't sure if she was pulling it shut behind her or opening it again so she could slip back inside to bed. But then an owl shrieked somewhere close by, making her jump, and the door clicked shut.

So she had to go.

"I was leaving anyway," Annushka whispered to herself as she stepped out into the snow. "I was."

She marched through the snow, her flashlight held tightly in her hand, making for the dark band of trees. She passed Eva's house and imagined her friend fast asleep, dreaming about tigers. If only she were like Eva, Annushka thought. Eva wasn't scared of anything—she was always so brave. She didn't care if people teased her or if she got scolded for being noisy at school. Eva had wanted to go and look for the tiger....

Annushka paused for a minute, wondering if she could throw snowballs at her friend's window and get her to come, too. But it would be too hard to wake Eva and explain, without waking her whole family. Annushka trudged on.

"The cub's probably still close by," she mumbled as the trees loomed up over her. "She could be just over there, waiting for the village to be quiet. She's probably hoping to come and find some food. I bet she can smell everyone's dinners.... I'll find her and give her some food so she follows me home, and then I can wake up Papa and he'll tell Dimitri. Then the people from the nature reserve will come and rescue her. Easy." Annushka swallowed hard. It was one thing to say it—but she still had to walk between those dark trees, in the middle of the night.

Like all the children in the village, Annushka knew how dangerous the forest was. It wasn't just the bears and lynx and wild boar that lived there; the place was vast. There were paths here and there, and hunters' huts. There were roads that cut through, as well as the train tracks that ran not too far from the village, but most of the forest was wild and empty. It was almost impossible to remember one's way—no matter hard Annushka tried, she was likely to get lost.

She fumbled in her coat pocket for her secret weapon—a ball of string. She wasn't sure how long it was, but it would give her a chance at least. Once she could no longer see the lights of the village, she would tie one end of the string to a tree. Then she'd be able to follow it back. It should help her see if she was walking in circles, too.

"String," Annushka muttered to herself as she stepped between the first of the trees, her flashlight beam shining on the dark-needled branches. "I'm hunting a tiger with a flashlight and a ball of string. Oh, and the *piroshki* from Papa's lunch."

The darkness seemed to close around her as she walked farther among the trees, but it felt a little warmer now that she was out of the wind. Annushka looked back. She could still see a few faint lights—it wasn't time to start unrolling the string yet. Those golden gleams among the trees were her last link to home, and she dreaded seeing them fade out. She had to keep picturing the tiger cub's golden eyes instead.

Annushka peered behind her and felt her heart thump. There were no more lights. She retraced her steps until she could see the village again and pulled the string out of her pocket. She could feel the little wooden tiger there, too; her fingers brushed it as she fumbled for the string. She smiled. It was her good-luck charm.

She unwound a length of string and looped it onto a low branch. She had to take her gloves off to get the knot to stay properly tied, and the cold bit at her fingers. Then she set off again, slowly unrolling the string behind her. Now it felt as though the journey had truly begun—that she was an adventurer.

Annushka shuddered.

"You're such a coward," she told herself angrily. "Think how scared the tiger cub must be, without her mother."

The string seemed to unravel horribly quickly—the ball was already a lot smaller, and she hadn't come far at all. What was she going to do when the string ran out? It had seemed like such a good idea when she saw it on the shelf in the kitchen. But would she really just turn back when the string was gone?

Annushka was so busy worrying about the string, and keeping her step on the rough, snowy ground, that it took a few seconds for her to notice the rustling behind her. She froze, hoping that it was the tiger cub—and that the strange connection she had felt between them wasn't something she had just imagined.

Slowly, she turned, lifting the flashlight to point in the direction of the rustling among the trees. All she could see between the pine branches was a lump of darkness—not the stripes of a tiger.

Annushka lifted the flashlight a little higher, and the light flickered and settled

on the face of a startled bear, its black fur gleaming in the beam of light. There was a clear ring of white around its throat, like a necklace. It was beautiful. But staring at her from between the bare branches of a silver birch tree, only a few feet away, it was terrifying, too.

Annushka stumbled backward, almost dropping the flashlight—and then she tripped, yelping out loud as she landed on her back in the snow. She was struggling to get up, hoping that the bear was as shocked as she was and she'd be able to dash away, when she heard more sounds, from behind her this time.

There must be two of them. How was she going to get away now? Annushka scrambled up to her knees, desperately searching for the flashlight. She'd dropped it as she fell, and it had gone out. Was it smashed? What if she had no more light? She was desperate to see what was happening.

At last she found the flashlight and frantically switched it on. The light shone and Annushka swung it around, trying to see what had made the new sound. She was expecting to see another bear, maybe even one rearing up and showing its teeth.

But instead, the tiger came padding toward her.

The little cub was even closer this time, close enough for Annushka to see the pink of her nose in the flashlight beam and the rich ruff of fur standing out around her face.

"Th-there's a bear!" Annushka stammered. She wasn't quite sure if she was warning the tiger or asking for help. The bear had looked so huge—was the cub big enough to scare it off? She wasn't much taller than Artur, the dog her grandfather had. But then Artur was a Samoyed, and he looked like a white bear himself.

Annushka wheeled around, waving her flashlight wildly as she tried to find the bear again. Was it coming closer? Would it attack?

The bear was still standing under the birch tree, but as Annushka watched, it slapped the ground angrily with one huge front paw and lunged forward a little way, clacking its teeth with a terrifying clatter.

Beside Annushka, the tiger cub snarled, gaping her jaws and twisting her ears back, her tail lashing. It was a stand-off, Annushka realized, as the two creatures stamped and snarled. Neither of them really wanted to fight, but they couldn't back down.

She watched, her heart thumping, as the tiger prowled forward, a low growl rattling the air around her. She was so brave but so little. Annushka could see how much bigger the bear was than the cub. Were bears scared of tigers? She just didn't know.

The bear began to back away, shaking its huge head uncertainly, and then all at once it turned tail and lumbered off, leaving Annushka and the tiger staring after it.

"You did it!" Annushka whispered delightedly. "You won!" Then she pressed her hand across her mouth to hold back a laugh. As the bear bounded away, its big bottom was bouncing up and down.

She turned to look down at the tiger again. "Are you all right?" she started to say, but then she realized—the tiger was gone.

Chapter
FIVE

Searching for the Tiger

Annushka looked around, confused. How had the tiger disappeared so fast?

"Where are you?" she groaned, stumbling through the trees, hoping to see a flash of orange fur or the gleam of golden eyes. But there wasn't even a glimpse of a tiger. Just a lot of scuffly marks in the snow.

"I was supposed to find you and bring you back with me. Or at least tell Papa and Dimitri where you are so they could call the nature reserve." She sighed. "I suppose you're still not that far from the village. That's good news."

The village.... Annushka looked down at her hands, holding the flashlight—only the flashlight. No string. What had she done with it? She shone the flashlight around the snowy forest floor, crouching and sifting anxiously through the piled snow. It must have fallen out of her hand when she tripped, she realized. And that had been ... where exactly? She'd forgotten and wandered on....

Her clever plan with the string was completely useless now. She couldn't see the lights of the village, and she had nothing to follow back home.

Annushka stood in the middle of a tiny snowy clearing in the forest and turned slowly in a circle. She had no idea which way to go, as the prints in the snow were all mixed up together. The only thing she could do was go on searching—the tiger cub had been just steps away. Annushka must be able to find her.

Strangely, she wasn't scared. There was something odd and dreamlike about this journey out through the night in the forest. It felt like a fairy tale. And in those stories, the child who was looking for something always found it in the end, even if there were twists and turns along the way. Annushka had set out wanting to save the little tiger, but so far it had been the tiger who had saved *her*.

"I'll go ... this way," Annushka muttered. The flashlight beam had landed on a tiny path, threading off between tall fir trees. It looked like it had been made by deer and the other animals of the forest.

She walked on, her footsteps crunching in the snow, turning the flashlight from side to side, searching for the tiger. The snow had drifted more thickly here, and her boots were starting to leave deep prints. She could see the trail of them, stretching out behind her. But just in front of her was another print, a perfect, round tiger paw print—and another and another, leading on ahead.

"Yes!" Annushka whispered delightedly, hurrying on after the tracks. She was sure that if she could find the tiger again, everything would be all right. Somehow, together, they would find the way home.

She clapped her hands together to keep them warm. She was glad of the layers and layers of clothes she'd put on—the night seemed to be growing colder, and it was definitely slowing her down. Each step seemed more of an effort than the last. It was so hard to keep walking when the view never seemed to change—trees all around her, trees ahead of her, a world of black branches and white snow.

The path began to open out, the tiger's tracks taking her into another clearing. A great tree had fallen—Annushka could still see part of its trunk under the snow—and next to it was a rundown little hut. It had probably been built from the wood of the fallen tree, she realized. It must be somewhere for hunters to sleep when they were spending the night out in the forest on a deer hunt.

She clapped her hands together again. Seeing the hut made her realize just how cold she was. Maybe she could go in and sit down for a bit. It would surely be warmer inside than it was out here. It was then she saw that there was smoke coming out of the chimney—and yes, there was a light showing around the cracks of the door. Someone was inside!

Annushka almost ran to bang on the
door, to wake them up and ask for help
finding her way back to the village. She
even hurried a few steps forward.

But then she realized that if she woke
the hunters, they would take her straight

home. The hunters would be horrified that she was out here all by herself—they wouldn't want to listen to why. And then the tiger cub would be alone and hungry again and it would all have been for nothing.

Tucking her gloved hands under her arms for extra warmth, Annushka turned away from the little hut and trudged on through the snow, following the tiger tracks. But she kept looking back at the safety and warmth she could have had, if only she'd knocked on the door.

It was getting harder to walk on now—her steps were even slower, and her head was thick and muzzy with cold. It was so tempting to sit down in the snow and rest.

"No," Annushka growled at herself. It was the cold making her think like that.

It was deceptive. If she sat down in the snow, she wouldn't get up again. But still ... the deep drifts were starting to look almost cozy.

Maybe she should eat the food she'd brought with her. Annushka stopped walking, blinking down at her coat. She had taken the *piroshki* that Papa had left in the fridge for his lunch the next day. He'd left them nicely wrapped up, and they fit perfectly in her deep coat pockets. She'd planned to be back in time to explain where they were.... She wasn't actually feeling hungry, but maybe the food would give her some more energy to fight the cold.

She patted vaguely at her coat, trying to find the foil packet, but her fingers seemed to be all thumbs. It was just too much effort to take off her two pairs of gloves, unbutton the pocket, and open up the wrapping. She was too tired. Instead, she clenched her fingers around the little wooden tiger tucked inside her glove and stomped on, one foot after the other.

She would *not* stop. She was going to find the tiger cub, she knew it, deep down inside her. It was so terribly important, and it all had to do with the little wooden tiger from Baba's mantelpiece....

Annushka blinked, her frosted eyelashes heavy, and then she shook her head. The wooden tiger was hers, carved by her papa. It had never belonged to either of her grandmothers. The cold really was making her dreamy.

She stopped for a moment to catch her breath and the flashlight shone on something ahead. Annushka peered forward, the strange weariness easing a little. What could it be? It looked like the glint of metal, but she couldn't think why there would be metal in the middle of the forest. She struggled toward it, realizing that the trees were thinning. It was a road, then—or no, the train tracks!

Annushka had come farther than she'd expected. The line ran past the village carrying passengers and goods to Vladivostok. She had traveled on it with her parents to visit relatives in the city. If she stayed close to the train tracks, she would come to somewhere with people. It might be a long walk, but she wasn't lost anymore.

Annushka took a deep, shuddering breath, at last admitting to herself how frightened she had been.

She stood looking at the track, wondering how far she could safely explore on either side without losing her way again. Would the tiger cub be frightened of the train tracks? she wondered. Or maybe it was a helpful landmark for tigers, too. Even if she went out of sight of the tracks, she would still be able to hear the trains, she realized. She could follow the sound back. Annushka stomped her feet up and down firmly, trying to ease her numbed toes. The track was so much more than just a set of rails and sleepers—it was a path and a sign. She felt awake now, and almost hopeful.

Annushka picked her way through the

piled-up snow on either side of the track and shone her flashlight along the metal rails. She was fairly sure she knew which way led back in the direction of her village. The tracks went past the village about a mile to the east, but she knew she could have lost her sense of direction in the forest. Once she had found the tiger cub, they would hurry back that way.

She rubbed her fingers over the little wooden tiger again and bit her cold-numbed lip. She still wasn't quite sure how she was going to get the tiger cub to follow her to safety. She kept remembering that moment when they had stared into each other's eyes, and hoping....

Annushka stomped her feet again—she had pins and needles. That was a good sign, she decided. Maybe it was getting warmer and the feeling was coming back to her feet. They were definitely buzzing, although it wasn't quite the same prickly feeling she'd had before. More of a low hum. Annushka wriggled her toes, and then she realized that it wasn't just her feet that were humming. All of her was.

A train! She was standing right next to the train tracks, and there was a train coming! The strange humming was the vibration of the wheels, speeding along the rails toward her. She glanced up and down the line, and far in the distance she saw the pinprick lights of the approaching train.

She was just turning to hurry back to the safety of the trees when her flashlight caught a dark shape huddled on the track. Annushka pointed the flashlight at it, hoping that it wasn't a fallen branch that might damage the train.

The flashlight beam shone back at her, reflected in the tiger's golden eyes.

Chapter
SIX

Befriending Star

Annushka let out a yelp of panic. The tiger cub was slumped on the tracks between her and the train. She dashed along the track, her boots skidding and clattering on the icy sleepers, and flung herself down beside the tiger.

"What are you doing?" she wailed. "Get up! You can't stay here ... look!"

The train was still quite a long way away, but it was approaching fast. Annushka figured she had less than a minute to get the tiger cub off the line.

"Are you hurt?" she muttered, pointing the flashlight at the cub. "Or maybe you're stuck? Do you have a paw stuck or something?" But all four paws seemed fine—the cub was just lying on the track, looking exhausted. As Annushka watched, the tiger's eyes closed again, and her head sank down on her front paws.

"You have to move ... come on!" she pleaded. The tiger had been so fierce and strong, facing off against the bear for her. How could she be so feeble now? Couldn't she feel the shiver of the metal underneath her? Didn't she know how much danger she was in?

The cub used up the last of her strength, Annushka realized. *She gave it all up to fight for me.*

"No," Annushka said grimly. She stuffed the flashlight into her pocket—she didn't need it as the lights of the oncoming train were casting an eerie white glow all around them now. Very soon, the driver would see her and the tiger, but Annushka wasn't sure he'd be able to stop even if he wanted to. The train was speeding toward them too fast.

She sucked in a breath, the freezing air stabbing at her throat. Then she wrapped her arms around the tiger's great chest and heaved. Nothing happened. Even though the tiger was only a cub, she was too big and heavy for Annushka to shift her.

"Just help me a little bit," she pleaded. "I came out here to save you. I'm not going to leave you here. I can't."

The tiger's eyes slitted open and she looked up tiredly at Annushka. Then the black tips of her ears twitched and she shook her head. Finally, she had sensed the danger she was in, Annushka thought. The tiger tried to pull herself up, her front legs shaking, but then she collapsed again.

Annushka bit her lip—the train was so close now that she could feel the shuddering of the rails all through her. Her fingers were actually trembling. But she scrambled up and dashed around to the other side of the tiger, crouching again to shove her from behind. "Come on!" she screamed, her voice lost in the thunder of the oncoming train. "Get up!"

There was a mighty shriek as the train driver caught sight of them on the tracks and sounded his whistle—as if they might not have noticed there was a train bearing down on them! But the blast of noise seemed to give the tiger the burst of energy she needed, and she scrambled up onto her feet with Annushka pushing behind her.

They lurched off the tracks in a stumbling rush and flung themselves clear. Annushka collapsed into the snow piled at the side of the tracks, her face pressed into the hot fur of the tiger's side.

She lay there watching as the train went past, as high as a house, wheels howling against the metal rails. It seemed to go on forever, so loud that Annushka trembled all over, sure that the very sound would shake her apart. She stared up at the quiet stars above them, holding onto their stillness in the thundering noise.

But what about the tiger? Annushka blinked and shook her head, and forced herself to look back down. The cub was stretched in the snow beside Annushka, her sides heaving. The lights from the train were flickering in her eyes, even brighter than the starlight.

"It'll be gone soon," Annushka gasped, or thought she did. She couldn't hear her own words. "It'll go, *zvezda moya*, I promise." She laughed weakly. *Little star.* That was what Baba called her ... and Papa and Mama. She blinked, confused for a moment. It was funny to say it to a tiger.

"Star," she said to the cub again, as the last carriages rattled past, leaving a trembling silence in the snow. She sat up slowly, expecting the tiger to dart away into the trees, now that the train was gone. But Star lay still, gazing back at Annushka, her golden eyes bewildered. She wasn't leaping up and dashing away like a wild tiger should.

"What is it?" Annushka asked. "Are you too tired to run?"

Or maybe the cub was just too scared to move, she thought worriedly. The train had been terrifying enough for *her*, and she knew what it was. To a tiger, it must seem like a great metal monster tearing through the forest.

She pulled her flashlight out of her pocket and shone it over the tiger, searching for wounds. It was hard to tell with such thick fur, but she couldn't see any blood. But ... the tiger cub's tail didn't look right, she realized, peering at it with a frown. Instead of orange fur banded neatly with black, and a black tail tip, the whole end of Star's tail was dark.

"That's frostbite," Annushka said, flinching a little. She remembered her grandfather showing her the stumps of his toes after she'd begged and begged, and how she'd then had nightmares forever afterward about her fingers falling off.

Star must have been so weak for her tail to freeze. Annushka shivered, imagining her collapsed in the snow, getting colder and colder. "You gave up and lay down," she realized. "Like I almost did. We have to get you some help. You need a vet." She sighed. It was silly, talking to a tiger as if she could understand, but then this whole night was starting to feel like a dream.

She put one gloved hand on Star's fat front paw and the cub sniffed at her feebly. "If you come back to the village with me," Annushka explained, "I could take you to

Dimitri. I bet he'd know what to do about your tail."

She glanced at the cub's tail again, dark and dead against the snow. A frostbitten tail wasn't going to get better.... She suspected that Dimitri would know exactly what to do with it, but she wasn't going to mention that to Star, just in case the tiger cub did understand her.

"Dimitri will figure out your tail, and then the people from the nature reserve will come and get you. It'll be so nice there—like a ... like a tiger home. But you're going to have to get up," she said encouragingly. "I know you can. You managed it before, when the train was coming."

But that had been because Star was scared—Annushka didn't want to frighten her into moving. She didn't know how to frighten a tiger anyway.

"This isn't going to work," she muttered wearily. "Maybe I should leave you here and walk back to the village on my own?" Annushka chewed her lip. Star wasn't moving now, but maybe when she'd recovered from the shock of the train, she'd wander off again. It was no good going and telling everybody she'd found a tiger if there was no tiger when they all came to find her.

"You *have* to come with me." Then she sat up, patting frantically at her pockets. "Papa's *piroshki*! They're chicken and mushroom! I bet you'd love them!"

Annushka pulled out the foil packet and started to fumble at it with her gloves. Her nose was too cold to smell the little chicken pies as she opened up the foil, but the tiger's whiskers twitched. Annushka tore off a piece of pastry and felt her stomach twist. She was hungry now, too, but not nearly as hungry as Star.

She wondered when the little tiger had last eaten. Had she managed to hunt at all since her mother had been killed? Or did she still not know how to? If she'd been desperate enough to come scavenging around the village, so close to humans, it was likely she'd just been eating the scraps of other creatures' kills—anything she could find. But whatever she'd been doing, she clearly had not been eating enough. Under her thick fur, the cub was skin and bone.

"Here, take this," Annushka said, holding out the piece of pastry. She tried not to flinch as Star reached for the tasty morsel, and the cub's yellow-white teeth flashed in the flashlight. Even a small tiger had very big fangs on either side of its jaw. But Star mouthed the pie out of Annushka's hand delicately, swiping the crumbs from the girl's glove with her huge pink tongue.

"Would you like some more?" Annushka asked, reaching for another piece. The tiger heaved herself forward, just a little, as though she were trying to rock back onto her paws and get up. She didn't quite manage it. Annushka clicked her tongue sympathetically and fed the cub the second piece of *piroshki*. Then she held the foil packet in front of Star's nose. "Look. There's a lot more. Come on."

This time, the tiger wriggled over so she was almost sitting up and pawed at the packet. Annushka giggled. "You see! You want them, don't you? Come on...." She shimmied back a bit, waving the pies temptingly.

The cub let out a frustrated little growl, almost a meow, and surged up onto her paws, lunging after Annushka and the *piroshki*. Annushka skipped away, hurriedly tearing off another piece of pie as a reward. "That's it! Come on, Star!"

The tiger stumbled after her, staring hopefully at the food, and Annushka started to feel as though her plan might work. The cub still looked tired and sick, but she was stomping along after those *piroshki* with an air of grim determination.

"I wish I could feed you the whole packet all at once," she said, waving a chunk of pie temptingly at Star, "but I have to make it last. I don't know how far it is back to the village. Or to somewhere they can call home for me. And I'm not sure how anyone's going to feel when I show up at their house with a tiger, asking to use the phone."

Star nipped the next piece of *piroshki* out of Annushka's hand and nudged at her gratefully. She was starting to look a bit more lively, which was good, but even that little nudge reminded Annushka how strong the tiger was. If she began to feel a lot better, Star could just knock her over and *take* the whole packet of little pies. There wasn't going to be any more of this nonsense about giving them out gradually.

Annushka moved a few steps ahead of Star and held up the *piroshki* a little higher. But the cub closed the gap at once and pawed hopefully at the packet, her claws raking the foil. If she stood on her hind legs, she would be as tall as Annushka.

"Okay, okay!" Annushka sighed. "Here you go. I'm just glad Papa packed up a lot last night. But once they're gone, they're gone." She handed Star a bigger bite of pie, and the cub snapped it greedily out of her hand. But when she landed again, whipping her tail eagerly, Annushka noticed her wince. The tiger looked back over her shoulder to glance at her blackened tail-tip, as though it were hurting.

Annushka hoped that was a good sign. Her grandfather had explained how frostbite worked when she was so upset about his toes. If Star's tail was painful, it meant it still had some feeling in it—there was still blood flowing, and the nerves were working. Maybe they were going to be in time to save it.

She nodded to herself, feeling more determined. The dazed, sleepy feeling that had been so frightening was almost gone—the excitement of finding Star and the terror of the oncoming train had given her a new energy to fight the cold. She couldn't let the little cub down. But they had to make it back to the village before Star collapsed again, or Annushka did.

Chapter
SEVEN

Finding Their Way

Annushka eked out the *piroshki* for as long as she could—but six little pies weren't much of a meal for a starving tiger, even if Star was only a cub. Much too soon, the food was gone, and Annushka figured they hadn't even walked a mile down the train line. Maybe less—it was so hard to tell when each step meant working their way through the thick snow. They were walking under the trees to make the going a little easier, but Annushka wanted to keep close to the tracks to make sure that she didn't get lost again.

Of course, if Star decided to go off on her own, Annushka would have to follow her. But the little tiger didn't seem to feel like wandering. She kept close to Annushka, even after the *piroshki* were gone. Annushka gave Star the empty foil packet to sniff, and the cub licked at the crumbs and then looked at the girl hopefully, clearly thinking she had more food.

Annushka held out her open pockets, so Star could see she didn't have anything else, and the tiger gazed at her for a while. Then she turned away and Annushka thought the cub was going to leave, but she didn't. She glanced back at Annushka expectantly, and Annushka realized she was waiting for her to walk on.

"Come on then," she said, her voice shaking slightly. She set off again and the tiger pressed in close by her side, so close that Annushka could feel the warmth of her as they walked on together. It helped— the wind was rising now, whipping up the snow and cutting through Annushka's thick coat.

"It's starting to get light," she said, peering up through the trees a little later. "I've been out almost all night." If the sun was rising, then her mama and papa were probably already up. They were always up in the dark in the wintertime. Sometimes Papa went out to the workshop before it was light. They would know that she was gone. She hadn't even left a note.

Mama and Papa and Peter and Tatiana would be running around in a panic, trying to figure out what she had been wearing and what she had taken with her. They might notice the missing *piroshki*, but probably not the ball of string.... Annushka swallowed, forcing down the lump of worry that had risen in her throat.

"We should walk faster," she muttered

to Star, leaning forward and pushing on through the deep snow. "They probably think you've eaten me...."

They quickened their steps, but the little burst of speed didn't last for long. Annushka had been up all night, and Star was sick and hungry. They couldn't keep going at any more than a stumble. Star was getting slower, Annushka realized. She wasn't pressed up close to her anymore; she was a few paces behind. The tiger was still walking, but her head was hanging down, and Annushka could see the effort it took to lift each heavy paw. She wasn't going to be able to walk for much longer.

"Do you need to stop and rest?" she asked, crouching down next to the cub. Hesitantly, she put one gloved hand on Star's furry ruff. She wasn't sure how a tiger would react to being petted, but Star didn't seem to mind. She pushed back against Annushka's hand the same way any other friendly cat would—but only for a moment. She looked exhausted.

Annushka glanced around at the trees, wondering if there were somewhere they could shelter for a little while. Even a fallen tree that would protect them from the wind—but all the trees were pines or slender birches, dark against the snow. There was nothing they could huddle behind.

"The sun's coming up," she told Star. "I'm sure it'll feel warmer soon. That'll be good...." It was definitely getting lighter—she could see farther through the trees than she'd been able to before. And there was a golden gleam cutting through the snow shadows that had to be the sunrise.

Annushka frowned at it and blinked, and then turned off her flashlight. Maybe it wasn't the sun after all. The sky was brightening around them, but this was different. It looked like ... a light.

"Another hunters' cabin?" she gasped, jumping up. "Star, come on! There must be someone there. They might have some food, and maybe they can call for help."

Annushka ran a few steps toward the light, stumbling in the snow, but then she realized Star was too tired to follow her. Hurrying back, she wrapped her hand in the tiger's thick fur and steered her forward, whispering encouragement to the little cub. "Look, it's so close. We're almost there, Star, I promise. Think of the food...."

But as they drew closer to the light, Annushka saw that it wasn't a hunters' cabin after all. The building was made of wood, but the roof was decorated with tiny, intricate turrets and domes, and the

walls were painted. It was a church set in a
tiny clearing in the forest, and the light was
a lantern hanging on the porch. Annushka
had seen it before from the train, the gilded
roof topped with a cross shining through
the trees.

"Oh.... Maybe not food." There wouldn't be anyone there this early, she guessed. "But we can rest on the porch for a little while. At least we'll be out of the wind."

The porch was almost completely enclosed, and the snow hadn't blown inside—it was almost dry. Annushka pulled back her scarf a little and patted Star, who was sniffing suspiciously at the locked door. It must smell like people, Annushka thought, and incense. Maybe candles. "It's all right," she whispered. "We're safe. You're going to be safe."

Out of the biting wind and huddled against Star's warm body, Annushka almost believed that was true. "We can't stay here too long, though," she told. "Just a few minutes to rest."

Star slumped down with her nose on her paws, and Annushka closed her eyes gratefully. She was so tired after a night of walking.

When she opened her eyes again, the sun was glittering on the snow. Annushka shook her head, blinking wearily and hoping that she had only slept for a few moments. But as she peered up into the sky, she could see that the sun was now high overhead, so it was mid-morning at least. They must have slept for a couple of hours—and Star was still asleep.

"Star...." Annushka shook the tiger cub gently. "Time to wake up." She giggled. She sounded like her mama. She ran her hand over the cub's neat ear and gently scratched at the soft tuft of fur behind it. Still the little tiger didn't move. She was curled up sideways, her head on her paws, and she seemed to be deeply asleep.

As Annushka rubbed the cub's ears, her head shifted slightly, tipping to the side and stretching out her white throat. Her tongue was sticking out a little, Annushka noticed. Annushka had been feeling very warm and comfortable, curled up next to a furry tiger, but now the cold seemed to hit her all over again, and somehow from the inside out.

What if Star *wasn't* asleep?

Annushka shook the tiger in a sudden panic, grabbing at the fur around the cub's head and pulling at her frantically. Star didn't wake up, but she did give a tiny huffing groan. Annushka sat back, panting, her heart thumping in her throat. Star was still alive, but she was unconscious—she *couldn't* wake up.

Annushka got to her feet, tucking her gloved hands under her arms, and stared down at the tiger. Star was sicker than she had been when they were on the train tracks. She was dying. Annushka had to get help for her ... now.

She looked out across the clearing. Should she go back to the train and walk on toward the village as fast as she could? The only other way to find people would be to go to the hunters' cabin—but by now, they would be out in the forest. And Annushka wasn't sure she could find the cabin anyway.

"I'll be back soon," she promised, crouching down again to whisper in Star's ear. "I'll be back soon with help."

Then she hurried out into the snow, plunging across the clearing and among the trees. The forest felt alive around her now—there were birds peering down at her from the branches, twittering warnings to each other. Something scuttled across the snow, leaving a floundering track. Annushka shivered, thinking of bigger tigers, and wild boar, and that black bear. She had felt so much safer with a tiger by her side, even if Star was only a baby.

She came out beside the train tracks and nodded to herself determinedly. She was going the right way—the little church wasn't that far from the village. All she had to do now was follow the track. Annushka trudged on, her head against the wind, counting her steps. She was fifty steps closer to finding help. A hundred steps closer. Five hundred steps. She stopped, looking back along the tracks—she could just about see the shadowy form of the church through the trees, now that she knew what she was looking for. It was horribly close still. Grimly, she continued counting.

She was at three thousand and

something steps along the track when she heard a noise—a shuffling, scratching in the trees that made her freeze with fear. She was sure it was the bear again. Slowly, she swiveled her eyes sideways, not wanting to draw the creature's attention to herself.

Annushka was expecting to see a great black bear looming among the trees, and for a moment that's what she saw—a bear, a huge one, even bigger than the young bear Star had saved her from. It was standing on its hind legs, dark and fearsome. But then she took another breath and the figure shimmered and settled ... but it wasn't a bear.

It was a human—a man, wrapped in so many layers of thick winter clothes that he looked as big as a bear. He hadn't seen her, Annushka realized. He was looking the other way.

"Hey," she called, but she was so surprised and relieved that it came out as a whisper. "Hey," she tried again, a little louder, and this time the man turned around.

Annushka could only see a tiny strip of his face above his scarf, just his eyes peering over at her in wonder, as though he couldn't believe there would be a child out in the forest. He actually leaned forward to look at her better for a moment.

Then he stomped forward, yelling over his shoulder, "Pavel! Nicholas! Come here!"

There was a chorus of grumbles behind him—the men were hunters, and their companion had just scared away all the game for miles. But then two other men appeared and stared at Annushka.

"What are you doing out here, little one?" the first hunter asked her. "Did you get lost? Are you with someone?" He looked around, as though expecting to see a whole family appear from the trees.

Annushka took a deep breath. This was exactly what she'd wanted to happen—the hunters would know the way back to the village, and they could take her and Star to safety. She didn't recognize the men, but the first hunter, the one with the reddish eyebrows, looked familiar. And even if they weren't from her village, they could take her there.

So why was it so hard to explain what she was doing, all of a sudden? "There's a t-tiger...," she stammered.

All three hunters tensed up and immediately reached for their rifles. Tigers might be protected, but they were also very dangerous.

"Must be the one that's been hanging around the village," one of them said, glancing at the trees. "Dimitri figured it had to be injured. Probably desperate, poor brute."

"No, no," Annushka squeaked. "I mean, yes, she is injured, but she's not dangerous, I promise."

"You've been close to her?" The first hunter came over to her, crouching down to look her in the eye. "Are you all right? Are you hurt?"

"I'm fine. Honestly." Annushka put her hand on his sleeve. She could imagine these three panicked men charging off into the forest to hunt down poor Star. "She's only a cub. Did you mean Dimitri the vet? He told my dad that he thought the tiger might be a cub whose mother has been killed, and he was right."

"You know Dimitri?" The hunter peered into Annushka's face. "Hey, are you Maria and Michael's little girl?"

Annushka nodded.

"You're in my son's class! And you're out here on your own? Your mama and papa must be frightened out of their minds, girl! We have to get you back home. How long have you been lost?"

"I'm not lost!" Annushka said angrily, drawing herself up straighter. "I came here to find the tiger cub, and I did!" Then she hesitated, suddenly unsure. A poacher had probably shot the cub's mother. What if these men wanted to do the same to Star? But Annushka needed help—the hunters were her only chance to get the cub back to the village.

She swallowed, and went on. "The tiger's at the church, not far away. She's lying down on the porch, and she's really sick. I think she's dying! Her tail's turned all black and horrible, and she won't wake up!"

"Really? There's a tiger cub at the church in the woods?" One of the other men shook his head wonderingly. "This girl went out to find a tiger, and she did...."

He turned to Annushka. "You're lucky to be alive!"

Annushka nodded. "I know. But please—you have to help me. She's too big for me to carry. I tried to pick her up when she was lying on the train tracks but I couldn't. You could carry her, though, I'm sure you could. If you put her on a blanket or something." All three men had packs—they must have something they could use.

"What do you think, Alexei?"

The first man nodded. "Show us, then. What's your name, little one? I can't remember."

"Annushka. Please hurry. I don't think she has very long."

"Annushka. Okay. Pavel, you call the girl's papa, if you have his number—or anyone back at the village. They'll all be out searching for her by now, I'm sure."

Annushka sniffed guiltily, imagining how worried her parents would be. It was for a good reason, but of course they wouldn't know that. She pulled at Alexei's sleeve again. "Please. We have to save the tiger and we're running out of time...."

Chapter
EIGHT

Help from the Hunters

Alexei turned toward the train tracks as though he were about to set off, but then Nicholas, the youngest of the three men, who hadn't spoken until now, shook his head and snorted. "This is some silly story the girl made up. How could she have found a tiger? We need to get her back home to her parents right away. If it was my Sofia, I'd be half dead with worry by now."

"It's not a story!" Annushka snapped. "Why would I make something like that up? I saw the tiger, and I could see she needed help!" She was clenching her hands into fists inside her gloves and glaring at the hunters. How could everything go wrong now, after Star had stood up to a bear and she had rescued Star from that train charging toward them? She couldn't let it happen.

"If you try and take me back to the village without her, I'll kick and scream every step of the way!" Annushka caught her breath. She needed that magic, that strange connection that had made her look for Star in the first place. She needed to make the hunters believe. But she didn't know how.

"Have you ever seen a tiger?" she asked Nicholas suddenly, and the young man gave his head a slow shake.

"She's beautiful. Her nose is pink—like ... like berries. And she has such fat furry paws. When she was asleep, curled up next to me, I think she was even purring. If you saw her, you'd want to help, I know you would."

The hunter shifted uncomfortably from

foot to foot and then glanced around at the others. "Oh, go on then, show us. I still think it's madness, not taking you right back home. But I suppose it isn't that far to the church."

Pavel tucked his phone back into his coat pocket, clapped his hands together, and nodded to Annushka. "You show us. And that was my neighbor. She's going to tell your parents we've found you."

"Thank you," Annushka whispered, turning pink under her scarf. She set off through the trees, beckoning them to follow her. "Come on. She's waiting for us."

The walk back through the snow seemed to take forever. Annushka kept thinking: *What if Star woke up and disappeared back into the forest?* But it was better than the other thought that kept sliding in after it: *What if we're too late? What if she couldn't hold on?*

Annushka's feet grew heavier and heavier with each step, but she stomped on, even refusing Alexei's offer of a piggyback ride.

"No. We're almost there. Look!" At last she could see the cross on the top of the little dome. She started to run, kicking up snow behind her as she fought her way on. "Please be there, please be all right, please be there, please be all right," she panted to herself over and over.

"There is something there...," Alexei muttered as they came closer. "The girl's right. My goodness. A baby tiger."

All three men stopped a little way back from the church porch to stare. It was as though they couldn't believe what they were seeing. But then Nicholas surged forward and crouched down beside Star.

"The little thing's half dead. We need to get her back to the village and the vet. Call Dimitri, Pavel. Tell him we're coming. Tell him to get stuff ready.

I think the girl's right, the cub has frostbite on the tail. She'll need some kind of drip. He'd better call that nature reserve and tell them we've got her, too." He glanced over his shoulder at the other two. "How are we going to carry her?"

"I'm wearing a fleece jacket under this coat," Alexei said. "Could we make it into a kind of hammock?"

"Oh, yes." Annushka nodded eagerly. "I can help carry her, too." For a moment she thought the hunters were going to laugh at her, but Alexei only smiled.

"She's heavy. We're going to need all the help we can get." Then he undid his jacket and took it off, shaking his head and muttering about how cold it was as he pulled off his fleece under-layer. He laid the fleece down next to the cub and eyed her thoughtfully, sucking his teeth.

Annushka knelt on the wooden boards and rubbed the top of Star's head. The little tiger didn't even twitch. "We could roll her over," she suggested, and Alexei nodded.

He looked cautious, as if he were worried Star would wake up and snap at him, but she didn't seem to notice as the hunters turned her onto the fleece. Then they gathered it up around her, Alexei and Pavel taking a sleeve each, and Annushka and Nicholas holding the hem, with the tiger's poor blackened tail trailing between them.

"Hope my old fleece holds up," Alexei muttered as they set off, following their tracks back through the snow. "She's heavier than I thought she would be."

Annushka had expected the journey back to the village to take hours. After all, she had walked and walked the night before, so she must have come a long way. But it was less than an hour later when she saw the shadows of houses through the trees, and then a figure came rushing toward her, sweeping her up in a hug.

"*Zvezda moya!* We thought we'd lost you!"

"Papa!" She hugged him back. "I'm sorry—I shouldn't have gone without saying anything—but ... but I had to...."

Annushka's papa looked down at her and then at Star, lying unconscious in Alexei's fleece jacket. He shook his head slowly. "It seems as if you were meant to find her. Maybe she was calling to you."

Annushka nodded. "That's what it felt like. It's all so strange. Like a dream." She blinked up at him in a daze, her mind suddenly crowded with other memories, ones that didn't fit. A tiger on the television news.... Her baba smiling down at her, in just that same way. But Baba was in the

United States, and Annushka hadn't seen her in so long. She shook her head.

"You should get her home, Michael. She's exhausted," one of the hunters said. Annushka was too dizzy to tell which one. She felt her papa pick her up, and she snuggled gratefully into his thick coat. But then she shook her head.

"No! Please, Papa. Let me go with them to Dimitri's clinic. I want to know if Star will be all right. She has frostbite; I'm so worried about her."

There were other people crowding around now, and Annushka realized Alexei was right—the whole village really had been searching for her. She could see Tatiana and Peter and Eva and the others dancing around and waving. Then her mama rushed up to hug her and kiss her and tell her she was never allowed to go out ever, ever, ever again, and then she kissed Annushka some more.

"You can wait until Dimitri has seen the tiger, and then you're coming home," her papa told her. "You need to sleep."

"And eat something," her mama put in anxiously. "Annushka, I can't believe you went out there all alone. Promise me you'll never do something like that again. Promise me."

"I promise," Annushka whispered, holding tight to her papa as the hunters carried Star into Dimitri's clinic. She was so tired now, and she couldn't imagine wanting to walk anywhere, let alone out into the forest. "I'm sorry I took your lunch, Papa...."

She blinked wearily, watching Dimitri listening to Star's shallow breathing, trying to find her heartbeat. "Will she be all right?" she asked him croakily, and the vet darted a smile at her.

"I hope so, Annushka. She's so lucky you found her—she wouldn't have lasted much longer on her own. I can dress her tail and put her on a drip to bring her fluid levels back up. The experts from the nature reserve are coming to get her. They were practically in the van before I'd put the phone down."

"Will her tail get better?" Annushka asked, wriggling out of her papa's arms and coming to stand by Star. The tiger cub looked so small lying on the metal table.

Annushka pulled off her glove and rested her hand in Star's thick rusty-orange fur. It was the first time she had touched the cub without her gloves on.

Dimitri sighed. "I don't think we can save the end of it—I'm sorry. But she's very young. She can grow up without it and I don't think she'll even notice by the time she's fully grown." Then he smiled. "Hey, look. The warmth is waking her up a little."

"Be careful, Annushka," her mama gasped, but Annushka hardly heard her.

Star had opened her eyes, her honey-golden eyes, and she was looking back at Annushka. Just looking at her, to say thank you.

Anna sighed and hauled the covers up around her ears. It was so cold. Almost as cold as it had been when she was struggling through the snowy trees.

Star! Anna sat up in bed, ready to jump out and rush to Mama and Papa to find out the latest news. Mama had whispered to her late last night that the van from the nature reserve had come to pick up the tiger cub—they had promised to call Dimitri and let him know how the cub was. She had been so sleepy that all she'd done was nod, and yawn, and snuggle back into bed. But maybe there was more news now?

She huddled the comforter around her neck like a cloak and padded across her bedroom floor in the half dark—and then stopped as the door opened.

"I was just coming to wake you, *zvezda moya.*" Baba was standing there laughing at her, holding a mug of hot chocolate. "I thought you might need this to help you get up—it's so cold. Have you seen all the snow? Your mama called, and she's coming to pick you up. There's no school today. Ruby wants you to go to her house to make snow angels." Baba tipped her head to one side, frowning at Anna. "What is it, little one? Are you sick? You look strange."

Anna shook her head. "I—I don't know. Maybe it was a dream." Had it been? She'd never dreamed anything so real before.... She had been *there*, and so had Star.... She had been in Annushka's house, she realized now. She had *been* Annushka.

"You were dreaming about the snow?" Baba smiled. "It's just like you wanted, isn't it? I told you!"

"Yes, you did…. I'll get dressed," Anna mumbled. "Thanks for the hot chocolate, Baba." She sipped at it slowly as she found her clothes—she only had her uniform with her, but she'd change at home.

The sweetness of the chocolate was helping her to wake up and the tiger dream was fading, the way dreams did. Anna gathered up her bag and stuffed her pajamas in it, and then looked around to make sure she hadn't left anything behind.

Lying on the floor next to her bed was a little wooden figure. A tiger—the one Uncle Michael had carved for Baba.

Anna sighed and sat down on the edge of the bed. So *that* was why she'd dreamed of a tiger and her cousin. That was all it was—a trick her mind had played on her because of the news program they'd watched and a tiny ornament. She sniffed and found that she was blinking away tears. She had so wanted it to be true.

Then Anna turned the little wooden tiger over in her hands ... and her breath caught in her throat.

The tiger only had half a tail.

When she'd gone to sleep the night before, clutching the little wooden figure, the tail had curled out behind the tiger in a heavy curve. She had imagined it swinging as the tiger loped along. She remembered it, for certain. But now the tiger's tail was only half there, and it wasn't broken—it had been carved that way.

"Are you ready, Anna?" Baba was

standing in the doorway again. "Your mama's on her way, and she'll make you breakfast at home. Oh, the tiger! Why don't you take him home with you, *zvezda moya*? An early Christmas present—you can keep him."

"Her...," Anna whispered. "It's a she. Can I really, Baba?" She wrapped her fingers tightly around the wooden Star and smiled up at her grandmother.

Whatever it had been—a dream, or a fairy tale, or some strange magic—Star was safe, Anna was sure. She would be out there in the forest again one day soon, her short tail flickering behind her as she padded through the snow....

BEHIND THE STORY...

Star really is out there in the forest, walking through the snow. Her name is actually Zolushka, which is the Russian name for Cinderella. She was found in December 2012 as a cub about three months old. Her mother had probably been killed by poachers, and Zolushka was left alone and starving. She was rescued by hunters, and the end of her tail had to be amputated due to frostbite.

But Zolushka's sad story has the happiest of endings. She was cared for by a rehabilitation center and kept away from humans so she could be released back into the wild at the Bastak Nature Reserve in the Pri-Amur region of Russia. Tigers had died out in the Pri-Amur more than forty years before, and Zolushka's rescuers were hoping to bring tigers back to the area.

In 2015, the tracks of two tigers walking together were found in the snow, and later that year, Zolushka was photographed with two tiny cubs of her own. It was the first time that a rehabilitated tiger had been released back into the wild and gone on to have cubs—an amazing wildlife success story.

The most recent photograph of Zolushka, from early 2018, shows her with another cub—she really is having a happy ending!

There's another tiger in this story—the wild tiger that Anna sees on the news at her baba's house, roaming around Vladivostok. Vladik is real, too—and he really did go exploring the city in October 2016. He was captured and taken to the same rehabilitation center as Zolushka and later released into Bikin National Park.

Vladik preferred his old territory, though. He was fitted with a GPS tracking collar at the rehabilitation center, so the scientists tracking him know he has actually walked out of the reserve and headed back the four hundred miles to the area around Vladivostok! He's been spotted crossing a road and walking across the train tracks. Luckily, he's had the sense to stay out of the city this time....

GLOSSARY

Baba—a shortened version of "babushka," which means "grandmother"; used mainly by children as a term of endearment

Piroshki—a small pastry with meat, cheese, or vegetable filling

Syrniki—slightly sweet, cheesy pancakes that are usually eaten at breakfast and served with sour cream and jam

Zvezda moya—a term of endearment; means "little star"

AMUR TIGERS

Amur tigers were once known as Siberian tigers, but sadly, these endangered big cats are no longer found in Siberia. They are now named after the Amur River, which runs through their habitat in the mountain forests of eastern Russia.

The largest of the wild cats, Amur tigers live alone in birch forests, easily camouflaged thanks to their stripes. They are powerful nocturnal hunters; they lie in wait until they see prey, such as elk or wild boar, then attack by pouncing.

SAVING AMUR TIGERS

The number of Amur tigers in the wild has decreased considerably due to deforestation and illegal hunting. But there are many efforts underway to save these majestic animals.

Organizations such as the World Wildlife Fund work with many companies and communities in a variety of ways. They help to keep a close eye on tiger populations; strengthen law enforcement to prevent illegal logging, which protects the tigers' habitat; increase the population of their prey; and raise public awareness.

SYRNIKI RECIPE

Make these Russian pancakes for breakfast or anytime!

What You Need

* 30 oz well-drained farmer's cheese or ricotta cheese
* 2 large eggs
* 1/4 cup granulated sugar
* 1/4 cup semolina or all-purpose flour
* 1 tsp vanilla extract
* Large mixing bowl
* Fork or mixer with paddle attachment
* Large ice-cream scoop
* Extra flour
* Oil or butter for frying
* Skillet

What You Do

1. Mix all ingredients in a large bowl using the fork or mixer. The mixture will be very sticky.

2. Use the ice-cream scoop to scoop some of the mixture and drop it into the flour. Roll into a ball and flatten into a 3/4" pancake. Coat the outside in flour as needed to prevent sticking.

3. Add oil or butter to the skilled and heat over medium heat. Fry the syrniki until deep golden brown on both sides. Add more oil or butter as needed to prevent sticking.

4. Serve with sour cream and jam or fresh berries. Yum!

Turn the page for an extract from…

WINTER JOURNEYS

THE
STORM
LEOPARDS

by HOLLY WEBB

Isabelle watched the group of children move off down the street. The pavement was slippery with frost and icy puddles, and one of the girls slipped and almost fell down. A couple of the others grabbed her to hold her up, and they all giggled.

If I were still back at home, I'd be out caroling with my friends, too, Isabelle thought. She closed the front door and leaned against it with a sigh. Some of the children from her old school went to the nursing home to sing carols at this time of year. Probably her friends would be doing that this week. Isabelle blinked at the Christmas cards hanging on a string along the banisters. Lucy had sent her one, and Ellie—really pretty, glittery cards, with long messages about how much they missed her and how school wasn't the same without her. And her friends had both made her laugh—she could almost hear them talking to her. But it was nothing like being back home with them, not really.

Isabelle had seen a couple of people from her new class when she'd opened the door—one of the boys had recognized her and waved, which was nice. But she still felt like an outsider. She hadn't been invited to join in. Nobody at this school knew that she loved singing.

"Wasn't that nice?" Isabelle's mom came back out of the kitchen, smiling. "I feel so Christmassy now!"

Isabelle nodded. She wanted to feel Christmassy, too. It was just that she felt so sad at the same time.

Her little sister, Tilly, was galloping up and down the hallway singing, "Dingle Bells! Dingle Bells!" and then neighing loudly. It was her favorite Christmas carol, but Tilly was only four, and she couldn't remember any more of the words.

"It's 'Jingle Bells, not Dingle Bells,'" Isabelle tried to tell her, but Tilly wasn't listening.

"There's no point," her mom whispered. "Come and have some hot chocolate. The carolling was beautiful, but it was cold standing at the door to listen. I wouldn't be surprised if it snowed soon—they did say it might on the news. That's one of the nice things about being farther up north now, isn't it? And I bet the snow stays cleaner here, too. It won't turn slushy and brown, like it does in the city."

Isabelle didn't say anything. She didn't think that the snow would make up for missing all her friends, and having to start at a new school a few weeks before Christmas. Her parents had explained everything to her and Tilly—how they were moving so Mom and Dad could run their own store instead of working for someone else. How exciting it was. And it meant they'd be living really close to Grandma and Grandpa. That was a good thing, Isabelle had to admit. But it was during a visit to Grandma and Grandpa's that her mom and dad had seen that the little cake shop they'd always loved was for sale. If only they hadn't walked down that street that day!

Isabelle's mom placed a mug of hot chocolate down in front of her, and then put an arm around her shoulders. "I know you're missing the things you'd have been doing back at the old house, Isabelle. But there are fun things happening here, too. It's the special Christmas event at the zoo tomorrow—with the reindeer, remember?"

Isabelle nodded and smiled at her. The hot chocolate was really good— thick and sweet, and Mom had even put marshmallows on top. She was trying so hard. But Christmas just didn't feel Christmassy here, even with the promise of snow.

Isabelle laughed as the penguin swam past, eyeing the visitors curiously through the glass panel set into the side of the tank.

Tilly danced up and down, squeaking, "Look, look, did you see, Belle? Did you see him? Do you think he likes my hat?" Tilly adored penguins—she was wearing her penguin hat and mittens, and she had been looking forward to seeing them all day, even more than seeing Santa's reindeer.

That was another good thing about their new home, Isabelle told herself firmly. The zoo was just outside of town, really not far away at all, and there were always special events and fun things to do. Her mom had said that they could come and visit a lot.

Tilly now had her nose pressed up against the glass, and she and Mom and Dad were all cooing at the penguins. Isabelle liked them, too, but the smell was getting to her.

"Mom…." She tapped her mom's arm. "Can I go and see what's on the other side of the path? That big enclosure with all the trees and rocks in it? I won't go wandering off, I promise."

Her mom glanced over at the tall enclosure, which looked as though it had been built around the side of a little hill.

"Okay, but be careful, please. Stay right there. We won't be more than five minutes; we'll catch up to you."

Actually, Isabelle thought, they don't have a chance of getting Tilly away from the penguins in five minutes, but she didn't say so. "See you in a bit," she told Mom and hurried up the steps from the penguin tank, glad to get away from the fishy stink. Probably at the South Pole penguins didn't smell as bad, she imagined. It was cold enough there to get rid of all the fishiness.

Once she was out on the path, the chilly wind blew the smell away, and she took a deep breath. Maybe Mom was right, and it would snow soon. The sky had that heavy, grayish-yellow look to it.

"Hello … Isabelle?" someone said, just behind her, and Isabelle spun around in surprise. The girl was so wrapped up in a big furry hat and a woolly scarf that it took Isabelle a moment to recognize her—it was one of the girls from her class at school.

"Hi," Isabelle said, a little shyly. Why couldn't she remember this girl's name? Daisy? Lottie? "Did you come to see the reindeer?" she asked.

The girl nodded. "Kind of. My riding school helps out with the Christmas parade that they have this afternoon. You know, with Santa Claus in his sleigh? The riding school lends all the ponies. I'm taking part in it, which is great, but I have to dress up in an elf costume. Promise you won't laugh at me!"

"Oh, I won't." Isabelle shook her head. "You're so lucky, going to a riding school. I've only been a couple of times on vacation—there weren't stables anywhere near our old house."

"You should come to Hill Farm," the other girl told her. "It's amazing. You could come with me the first time, so you weren't all by yourself."

"Daisy! Come on!" A man was waving at them, and Daisy grinned at Isabelle. "Got to go. I told my dad I'd only be a minute. I just wanted to say hello. See you later! Remember—promise you won't laugh at my silly costume!"

"I won't!" Isabelle smiled and watched as Daisy dashed away. Riding stables, close by! And Daisy had said Isabelle could go with her—she'd really sounded like she meant it, too. Isabelle walked over to the enclosure, still with a smile on her face, feeling better than she had in days.

Also by HOLLY WEBB:

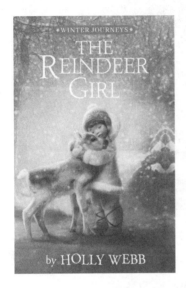

HOLLY
WEBB

Holly Webb started out as a children's
book editor, and wrote her first series for
the publisher she worked for. She has been
writing ever since, with more than 100 books
to her name. Holly lives in England with her
husband, three children, and several cats who
are always nosing around when she is trying to
type on her laptop.

For more information
about Holly Webb visit:

www.holly-webb.com
www.tigertalesbooks.com